Poppy and Prince

Kelly McKain

Other titles in the series:

Megan and Mischief

Chloe and Cracker

Sophie and Shine

Charlie and Charm

Emily and Emerald

Lauren and Lucky

Jessica and Jewel

Hannah and Hope

And coming soon:

Millie and Magic

www.kellymckain.co.uk

THIS DIARY BELONGS TO

Poppy

Dear Riders,

A warm welcome to Sunnyside Stables!

Sunnyside is our home and for the next week it will be yours too! We're a big family - my husband Johnny and I have two children, Millie and James, plus two dogs ... and all the ponies, of course!

We have friendly yard staff and a very talented instructor, Sally, to help you get the most out of your week. If you have any worries or questions about anything at all, just ask. We're here to help, and we want your holiday to be as enjoyable as possible - so don't be shy!

As you know, you will have a pony to look after as your own for the week. Your pony can't wait to meet you and start having fun! During your stay, you'll be caring for your pony, improving your riding, enjoying long country hacks, learning new skills and making friends.

And this week's special activity is a great day out at Western Bob's Ranch, so get ready to ride 'em cowgirl! Add swimming, games, films, barbecues and a gymkhana and you're in for a fun-filled holiday to remember!

This special Pony Camp Diary is for you to fill with all your holiday memories. We hope you'll write all about your adventures here at Sunnyside Stables - because we know you're going to have lots!

Wishing you a wonderful time with us!

Jody xx

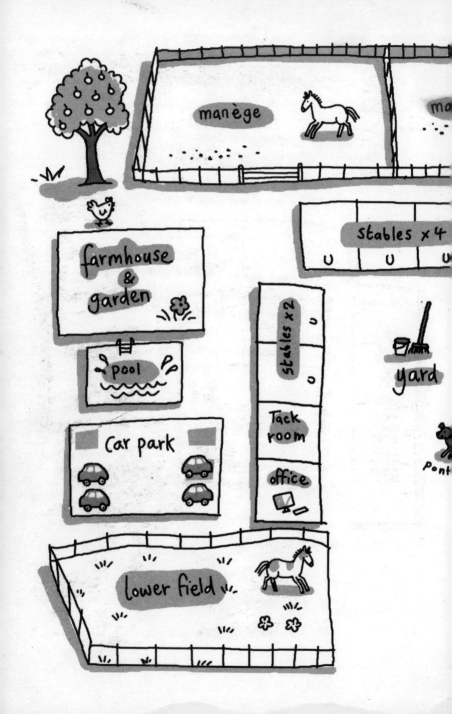

Sunnyside Stables

Monday, at Pony Camp!

Jody's just given me this special diary to write down all my adventures at Sunnyside Stables. I'm so glad to be here, it looks like such a great place – and I'm really excited about riding for the first time in weeks. On the way in I saw a field full of lovely ponies and I couldn't help trying to guess which one will be mine! But I'm also feeling very nervous because I don't know if I'll even dare get on her (or him!).

That's because two months ago I had a fall at my local riding school. They were holding a show jumping competition and I'd entered the novice class on my fave pony, Pepper. I went clear in the first round, and I really wanted to win, but in round two I got my strides wrong and jumped the combination a bit long. Pepper clipped the second set of poles and nearly fell over – and I came flying off and smacked right

into the wing, then landed strangely on my
arm. When I got up, it was hanging
at a funny angle – turns out it was
broken! It should have really hurt
but at the time I couldn't feel anything.
Mum said later it was probably because of the
shock. When the pain did come on, it was
terrible. Two first-aiders made me a sling and
helped me out of the manège, and then Mum
took me to casualty. I didn't get back on Pepper
that day, of course. And my arm took six weeks
to heal.

But the fall isn't really the problem (my arm's
fine now) – it's what it has done to my
confidence. I did try to have a lesson at my
stables last week, to get used to things again, but
I didn't even manage to get on. I just couldn't
make myself do it. It was awful because all the
helpers, Hayley (my instructor) and Mum were
standing there saying encouraging things, but I

was really dizzy and trembly. In the end I ran off to the loo, pretending I wanted to be sick. And then I stayed in there for ages just feeling so silly and weedy, until Mum banged on the door and took me home.

Right now, I'm sitting on a bench outside the office, which is next to the tack room. There are stables round all three sides of the yard and a gorgeous (and massive) carthorse is peering out at me! It's really cool here because there's a swimming pool (I love swimming) and also these sweet black labs called Viola and Cello, who gave me a big licky cuddle when I arrived! So even if I don't dare to ride this week, I'm sure I can help out on the yard and play with the dogs and do swimming and stuff – so I'll still have fun. Just hanging around here will be fantastic, and maybe the pony I'm given for the week will help me get back in the saddle again!

11

I know I shouldn't eavesdrop but I'm desperately trying to hear what's going on in the office, because Mum said she would have a word with Sally and Jody about me losing my confidence. I feel squirmy with embarrassment about her telling them, but I'm also relieved because if they know, they can help me get back to riding. But – urgh! – I've just had a horrible thought. What if they say, "Oh yes, yes, we understand" to Mum, and then when she's gone they get cross with me if I get scared and don't want to do things? And what if I *can't* get back on and the other girls all laugh?

Oh, it's just so annoying that this has happened! I wish I could

but I can't.

But maybe it will be easier here because no one knows what I was like before the fall. It's weird to think that I've got a stack of rosettes at home, for show jumping comps and dressage tests and one-day events. Nothing scared me!

But there's no way I'm telling anyone here that, because then they'll expect me to be really good. And just now I'll be happy if I can even *sit* on a pony!

This lovely girl Lydia has just now asked me if I want to help her pick out Phillip the carthorse's giant feet. If everyone here is as nice as her I should be fine. Right, no more being scared — I've decided that Sunnyside *is* the perfect place for me to get back in the saddle. I'm going to get on — today!

Still Monday,
before the first lesson (gulp!)

My new room-mates have gone down to the yard, but I'm hanging around up here to quickly write what's happened so far.

When everyone came out of the office, Sally spotted me helping out with Phillip and gave me a big smile. "Don't worry, Poppy, we'll get you riding again," she said. So she's nice too – phew! I asked her not to tell anyone else about the fall or about me being so nervous now, and she promised – thank goodness. I don't want anyone feeling sorry for me.

The other girls all started arriving then so I thanked Lydia for letting me do Phillip's feet and followed the crowd upstairs. I'm sharing with this girl Jennifer who has a gingery-brown bob with flicky-up ends. Her suitcase is huge – I think she's brought everything she owns! Our room is actually Millie's own bedroom (Millie is Jody's daughter) and it's really nice of her to share it with us. Millie has her normal bed by the window and me and Jennifer are in the bunk beds. I said I didn't mind which I had so Jennifer chose the top one. (I was secretly hoping for that one too but making friends is more important!)

They both seem nice, especially Millie, but I think I might have a BIG problem keeping my fall a secret.

When we were unpacking, I kept glancing at Millie and thinking, "I KNOW that girl." And then suddenly I worked out where from. We've both competed in a local show jumping competition – and I beat her! From the second I realized, I was just desperately hoping she wouldn't recognize *me*, but she soon said, "Haven't I met you before, Poppy?"

I wouldn't usually lie, but I didn't know what to do, and I found myself saying, "Erm, no, I don't think so."

Millie said, "Well, in that case you've got a twin out there who beat me and Tally at the Crewkerne show!"

I made myself grin and reply, "Really? That's

Luckily we got distracted by Jennifer telling us all about her last show jumping competition and re-enacting her fabulous victory. It sounded amazing (almost too amazing to be true, actually). Then she said she could canter a circle on the spot in dressage and Millie instantly cried, "No way! I don't believe that's possible even if you are really, really good unless you're a grown-up professional with a specially trained horse and everything!"

 Jennifer looked kind of surprised and embarrassed at the same time. She mumbled, "Well, I haven't actually DONE it yet, but I read about it in *Pony* mag and I reckon I could with a bit of practice."

"Yeah, right!" Millie scoffed. She's so pony-mad she can spot a fib a mile off. Urgh! – I hope she doesn't spot mine!

Jennifer was a bit sniffity after that. She turned on me and demanded, "What have YOU done, then?" I just completely panicked and blurted out, "Oh, you know, the usual." Then I added, "Hey, I love your fleece," to change the subject.

But Jennifer kept on at me, asking, "But like what, though?"

I went all red and flustered then, like I do in maths when I've been daydreaming and Mr Raines asks me a question. I carried on unpacking and mumbled, "Erm, walk and trot, obviously, some canter and a bit of jumping."

$16\% \text{ of } 100 = ?$
$3/4 + \frac{1}{2} = ?$
$75 + 21 = ?$

"Oh," she said, "So you're—"

"But only a tiny bit of jumping — pole work mainly," I added quickly, in case she started asking about heights and combinations and all that.

Jennifer just gave me an unimpressed look and turned back to her bulging suitcase. Phew! I think I got away with it! Of course, I wanted to reveal the truth and shout, "Actually, I *am* the girl from the Crewkerne show and I've even done cross country and a Pony Club team dressage competition – so there!" But I kept quiet.

Me at the Crewkerne show where I beat Millie and Tally!

Oh, Jody's calling me down to the yard now. Time to meet my pony (hurray!) and see if I dare ride again. Help!

Still Monday, after lunch
- there's just so much to say!

I GOT ON! Thanks to my *amazing* pony!
He's called Prince, and I already love him to bits.

When we'd all gathered on the yard, Jody
introduced herself together with Sally and Lydia
(she's the nice girl I've already met, and we're
supposed to ask her if we need help tacking up
and things).

Then all us riders got to meet each other too.

There's a beautiful Indian girl called Amita
who's about 15, and she's sharing a room with
these two friends who've come down from

London together, called April and Amanda —
I think they're both about 13.

Amita

April

Amanda

Then there's me and Millie and Jennifer…

Millie

Me!

Jennifer

…and lastly some younger girls — Sophie and
Tess and this girl Lucinda who's brought her
own pony with her, a grey Welsh Section A
called Lovely.

Sophie

Tess

Lucinda

Then it was time to meet our ponies!
As Lydia led them out there was a lot
of squealing and patting and fussing,
which made me just feel more and more
excited. Then Sally winked at me and said,
"We've got the perfect pony for you, Poppy,"
and out came my gorgeous Prince, a fairly
cobby piebald with a really sweet face.

Sally handed me the reins, saying, "Prince is
patient and honest, he'll look after you."

I made a big fuss of him, patting him and
stroking his muzzle. Then I whispered, "I'm very
nervous, Prince. I haven't been on a pony since
I had a bad fall. You
really *will* look after
me, won't you?"
Prince pushed his
nose against my
hand and I just knew
that meant yes!

Then suddenly Jennifer was shrieking with excitement, and Sally was telling her to calm down or she'd spook the ponies. She'd got this beautiful chestnut mare called Flame, who is about 14hh, with a lovely blaze. She wasn't very keen on standing still, and kept trying to barge past the other ponies.

Sally said to Jennifer, "Flame can be a bit of a handful, but I'm sure you'll be able to manage her with all your experience."

Jennifer looked really proud and said, "No problem!"

When everyone had got their ponies, Jody explained that they'd been tacked up for us today but from tomorrow we'll be doing it ourselves. April and Amanda were panicking because at their riding school it's all done before they arrive, but Sally told them not to worry as we'll be having a lecture and some practice this afternoon. I offered to help anyone who was stuck, and Sally said, "That's very kind of you, Poppy." Then Jennifer offered too, in a very loud voice, and she looked really cross when Sally just gave her a smile instead of answering. Jennifer's nice and everything, but I am starting to think she's one of those people who like to be the centre of attention. Well, that's fine with me, because I don't!

As the others queued up for the mounting block, I dithered about and made sure I was at the back of the line. When it was my turn, I found myself fiddling with Prince's numnah even though it was perfectly fine. My heart was pounding like hoof beats and I felt really sick. It seemed as if everyone was staring at me and I had to tell myself firmly that they couldn't be, because only the staff knew about my fall. For a moment I just wanted to drop Prince's reins, bolt back inside and hide under my duvet. But then I thought back to how determined I'd been earlier on. I'd absolutely promised myself I'd mount. Then Prince lowered his head and nuzzled me and that was all the encouragement I needed – I had a gorgeous, kind pony and I was determined to ride him!

Just then Lydia came over and gave me a big smile. "Up you go, Poppy," she said cheerfully. "I'm right beside you. I won't let Prince go anywhere." She took the reins and I climbed on to the mounting block. I still felt sick and trembly, but I knew I had to try. I took a deep breath and put my foot in the stirrup, then I bounced a couple of times, and suddenly I was on! "Well done!" cried Lydia. "Will you be okay now?" I nodded and so she went off to help Tess check her girth.

Me on Prince!

Then something really embarrassing
happened. While I was still adjusting my stirrups,
Prince started walking forward, following the
group into the manège. It should have been no
big deal but I panicked and before I could stop
myself I cried out, "Sally!"

Everyone turned round to stare at me and I
went all red and flustered. Sally came over and
told me to stay calm, adding, "I'll be watching
you, and remember what I said – you can
always trust Prince." Then she asked Lydia to
put me on the lead rein. I felt a bit better then,
despite Jennifer's raised eyebrows.

Once I got used to Prince's plodding rhythm
and realized that he needed a little squeeze
every other step just to keep him going, I began
to feel relaxed. He definitely wasn't going to
cart me off across the school – thank goodness!

We practised walking on and halting for a
while, and everything started to feel really

natural, like it used to. But when Sally said we were going into trot, I completely tensed up and I didn't want to squeeze on with my legs. Lydia said, "Stay relaxed, Poppy, you're doing really well. You can always put the reins into one hand and hold the pommel if you feel unsteady."

I felt tears welling up then and when I squeezed my eyes shut to stop them, my mind flashed up an image of all the rosettes on my wall at home! That's when I thought, *There's no way I'm holding the saddle!* I gathered my reins, took a deep breath and squeezed on, determined to try. Prince made a good transition but I just went all stiff and bobbled about with my hands in the air!

me looking v. silly

Sally called out, "Relax, Poppy! Your legs are saying go but your hands are saying no!" The rhyming made everyone giggle (including me!) and I felt a tiny bit better. When I finally got a nice rising trot going it felt great. I couldn't believe I'd done so much in one lesson, even if it was with a leader. Sally said I could come off the lead rein this afternoon, and I must have looked scared because she laughed and added, "You'll be fine, Poppy, but of course, you can go back on anytime you like."

I made a big fuss of Prince in the yard as we all dismounted, and I whispered in his ear, "Thanks for keeping me safe and trying so hard. Maybe next time we'll be able to do it all on our own!"

I love Prince – he's so gorgeous. Sally was right, he *is* the perfect pony for me!

Still Monday, after tea (chicken, jacket potatoes and green beans - yummy!)

Millie and Jennifer are on after-tea cleaning up duty so I've got our room to myself – well almost to myself! I'm glad I got the bottom bunk now because Cello is on my bed and I don't think I could have lifted her up to the top.

This afternoon we helped skip out the stables and refill the water buckets – it's so great to be on a yard again. Then we had our Tack Lecture with Jody, and a practice on April's pony, Charm, a handsome grey Connemara. When we were doing "parts of the saddle", I kept putting my hand up and I was even getting the hard things right, like the skirt and the D-ring, which not everyone was sure of.

I was really enjoying myself and feeling like the old pony-mad Poppy when Sophie, the little blonde girl who's got Monsoon, said, "Wow, Poppy, you know loads for a beginner!"

pommel
skirt
cantle
D-ring
seat
knee roll
stirrup iron
stirrup leather →
saddle flap

I felt myself go all red and hot again. I never actually *said* I was a beginner! They just think that because I had a leader in the lesson! "Yeah, erm, well, I read loads of horsy books," I mumbled.

After that we did "parts of the bridle", but I was careful not to answer too many of the questions. Jody kept looking over at me when no one knew the different nosebands and I kept pretending to have to adjust my left boot so I didn't catch her eye. She knew I was holding back, but she's so nice she didn't say anything.

It was great tacking Prince up all by myself
– it felt as if he was my very own pony.
Then Jody asked me to give Tess a hand
with Tiny and I helped her do the thumb-in-
the-corner-of-the-pony's-mouth thing to get the
bit in, because she was quite scared about it.
(Tiny's a cheeky little monkey!) I said, "You'll get
it with practice, there's just a knack." And then I
remembered that they think I'm a beginner and
quickly added, "That's what I read, anyway."

When I went back to get Prince and lead him
out to the mounting block he was giving me a
look, like he thought I should have told Tess and
Sophie the truth about my level of riding.

"It isn't lying, Prince," I whispered to
him. "I just don't want people to expect
too much from me – not while I'm getting
my confidence back!"

He snorted and pushed my hand with
his nose, so I knew he understood after all.

For the afternoon lesson I was put into Group A, which I knew straight away was the beginner group, because Millie and Amita are in Group B (and so is Jennifer). "You'll all still go on hacks and trips together," Sally explained, "but having two groups for lessons makes it easier for each rider to get the level of attention they need, and to make the most progress possible."

In the lesson I tried to relax and keep my head up and my hands down. I really wanted to ask for a leader, but instead I took some deep breaths and kept Prince moving with my legs, and soon I felt much better. When we were going into trot I couldn't help lifting my hands and tensing up, though. Sally called out, "Just trust Prince, Poppy."

That made me relax a bit and I found my rhythm and went rising. We did some circles and bending work around cones in walk and trot and then Sally said we'd try a canter to the back of the ride for those who wanted to. I felt really panicky and didn't think I could – after all, I was cantering when I came off! Sophie wasn't too sure either, as she really is a beginner and has only just got the hang of rising trot.

"Hands up if you want a go!" called Sally, but me and Sophie kept our hands firmly down. Sally smiled at us and said that was absolutely fine and got us to turn our ponies into the middle so we could watch. Lucinda cantered Lovely round the track and they looked really good, apart from a little wobble when she went back to trot. And then *Tiny* cantered *Tess* round the track! Tess flopped forward and only just managed to hang on, but Sally still said she'd done brilliantly! Sophie looked at me with this big grin on her face and said, "I'm *definitely* trying next time. Aren't you, Poppy?"

"Erm, yes," I said. "Definitely." But to be honest it looked so fast and scary, I can't imagine ever cantering again. I feel so cross with myself for being such a scaredy-cat — it's not like me at all, but I just can't seem to help it.

On the way out of the manège, Sally gave Prince a big pat and told me how well I was doing. "But I didn't even canter," I said glumly.

Sally smiled. "Poppy, it's only the first day," she cried. "You're off the leader and you've got a nice trot going, when you didn't even expect to get ON! It won't be long before you're back up to speed. Don't be so hard on yourself."

I nodded and smiled, then rode Prince into the yard feeling much better. But not for long, because a moment later Jennifer's group came in. "We cantered without stirrups!" she announced. "What did you lot do?"

Lucinda and Tess were excitedly telling her how they'd cantered but I had to admit that I hadn't. Jennifer looked really sorry for me and said loudly, "Don't worry, Poppy, I doubt Prince has got a canter in him anyway. He's so dopey. I'm sure it wasn't your fault."

I can't *believe* she said that right in front of my gorgeous pony. I got really annoyed then and snapped, "He's not dopey, he's just gentle! He'd go for it if I asked him to. I just, erm, didn't feel like it today, that's all."

Jennifer said, "Well sor-ry, I was only trying to be nice!" and clip-clopped Flame off to her stable in a huff.

When she'd gone, I gave Prince a big cuddle,

and told him to ignore her. "It's not your fault we didn't canter, it's mine," I whispered. "I bet you really wanted to go for it! I'll try next time, I promise."

So I HAVE to canter now, because Prince is really looking forward to it!

Oh great, it's time for our Evening Activity – swimming. At least that's something I can do without getting scared!

Tuesday at 7.11am
- up early and writing this while the others are still asleep!

We had such a great time in the pool last night!
First Millie's dad, Johnny, organized some fun
games like relay swimming and musical floats.
Then we had some time to play on our own so
me, Millie and Jennifer did diving down to the
bottom to pick up coins. Jennifer kept coming
back up empty-handed and spluttering, which
was funny after she boasted about being the
captain of the swimming team at her school!
Millie was giggling and singing "pants on fire",
and I joined in – but Jennifer went all red and
cross and didn't see the funny side, so we
stopped. Inside I was thinking, *What if Millie finds
out I'm a big liar too?* I still felt awful about
pretending I wasn't at that show with her.

But I didn't have to feel bad for long. Jennifer finally stopped being cross about the singing, and after lights-out we were all giggling and whispering silly jokes and I sort of forgot how annoying she was earlier. Instead it was as if we had all been friends for ages.

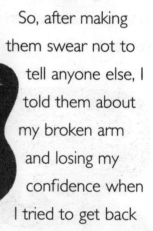

So, after making them swear not to tell anyone else, I told them about my broken arm and losing my confidence when I tried to get back on Pepper last week, and how I did know Millie after all. I kept saying, "Sorry, sorry, sorry," to her but she just giggled and promised that it was okay and she understood – phew!

"So you haven't got a spooky twin then?" she teased.

"No!" I cried, giggling and blushing.

The only bad thing was that Jennifer seemed to think she'd have been fine after a fall like that. (That's when I remembered that she actually IS annoying!) She kept saying, "You should have got straight back on, Poppy. That's what they say, isn't it? Get back on as soon as you can. That's what I'd do."

Millie pointed out that she couldn't know for sure what she'd do until it happened, but Jennifer insisted that she'd just leap back on.

"I tried," I wailed. "I didn't expect to feel this way. While I had the cast on my arm, all I did was look forward to riding again — but when it came to it, I…"

I trailed off then, feeling upset inside because it seemed like Jennifer was calling me a weed, and I suddenly started missing Mum. But I cheered myself up by thinking of how kind and understanding Millie was, and also by hugging my unicorn, Waffle, who I'd brought from home.

Oh, Millie's alarm has just gone. Got to go — time to start a totally fab new pony-filled day. I just hope I can keep my promise to Prince about the cantering!

Tuesday, after lunch, sitting on the bench in the yard

Oh, dear — this morning has been awful!

It started off okay because we got our ponies in from the field and my gorgeous Prince came straight up to the gate to meet me! He is just so lovely! But then we had our ponies tied up in the yard where Sally and Lydia could see us, and we were all chatting away as we got on with grooming, and that's when everything went wrong. I suddenly noticed that people were whispering something secret to each other. I thought someone would tell me too, but no one did.

I looked over at Jennifer and smiled. She smiled back but she didn't come over and say anything in my ear, like she'd just done with Sophie and Lucinda. Then I started chatting to

Sophie, who was scrubbing out feed buckets by the yard tap. I said, "I really hope we can try a canter today. It'll be great, won't it?"

I was so shocked when she gave me an angry look and said, "How could you pretend to be a beginner like me when you're not? You've cantered loads of times!"

I just stared at her as she stormed off across the yard. Then I realized – the whispering was about ME. Jennifer had told my secret!

My stomach started churning and I felt all empty and strange – how could she?!

I went marching up to her and said, "You promised you wouldn't tell!" I knew that everyone else was watching and straining their ears to listen, but I didn't care. I was too angry to be embarrassed.

"I was only trying to help," she said, matter-of-factly. "Now everyone knows, we can all support you."

"Well, thanks," I hissed, "but that's not really the point, is it? You PROMISED not to tell."

Jennifer just looked impatient and started grooming Flame's shoulder. I was so angry I had to stop myself from snatching the brush out of her hand.

"I don't know why you're making such a fuss," she said casually. "And by the way, you really should challenge yourself and have a canter today. You simply must get back up to speed or you'll lose all the skills you worked so hard for. Sally's being far too soft on you."

REALLY ANNOYING!

I just couldn't believe it! My heart was pounding so hard I could feel it in my ears. I wanted to run to Millie, but she was inside catching up on her holiday homework. Instead, I hurried back to Prince, untied him and walked him right round to the other side of the yard. Then I put him next to Charm and Fisher, April and Amanda's ponies, and got on with my grooming.

"Are you okay?" asked April. I swallowed hard and nodded. I didn't trust myself to speak, in case I started crying.

"Don't worry about Jennifer," said Amanda. "She was only trying to help."

My eyes filled up with tears then so I quickly turned away from them, pretending I'd spotted some stubborn mud stuck to Prince's foreleg.

"She is NOT just trying to help," I told Prince, as I struggled with the knots in his shaggy mane. "She's trying to ruin my holiday!"

Prince gave me a sympathetic look and I knew that he understood. I was determined not to let Jennifer spoil things for me, but when we mounted up ready for our first lesson, Sophie called out, "Shouldn't Poppy be in Group B, Sally?"

I wanted the ground to open up and swallow me – and Prince too!

I went all red and flustery and tried to pretend I didn't hear what

The ground swallowing me up!

Sally was saying to the other girls, which was, "Poppy is doing just fine where she is."

As Jennifer rode past me to join her group, she said, "Don't worry, Poppy, no one thinks you're a weed. Everyone just feels sorry for you."

"But I don't WANT them to feel…" I started saying, but she'd trotted off.

45

After that I couldn't think about anything except what Jennifer had said, that I MUST canter. I got more and more anxious as the lesson went on, and when it was time to canter, Sally gave us the choice again and Sophie eagerly said she'd have a try. I said I would, too, but then suddenly the tears were spilling out.

"Poppy, it's fine not to!" said Sally, smiling kindly.

"But I have to canter today," I insisted, gulping down the tears, "or I'll lose all the skills I've learnt and NEVER get my riding back!"

"What a drama queen!" Sally cried. "Is that what you really believe?"

"Well, I… It's just, that's what Jennifer thinks," I admitted.

I thought Sally would be cross with me, but instead she just laughed and said, "Well! I thought *I* was the riding instructor round here, but I must have got it wrong. It's obviously Jennifer!" That made me giggle, but then she went all serious and added, "Only do things when

Jennifer ↘ INSTRUCTOR!

you feel ready, Poppy. And, as I said before, trust Prince. If you're relaxed and confident and he understands what you're asking for, he'll always try. He's a wonderful pony."

I ruffled his mane and said, "I know. In fact I wish he was really mine and I could take him home after the holiday."

Sally patted his shoulder. "Oh, no," she said, "you can't have him. He's got an important job to do here, helping riders find their feet again. You'll always love him, I'm sure, but you won't always need him."

I nodded, but I don't believe her at all. I can only ride patient, perfect Prince. There's no way I could manage on any other pony. The thought of getting on fiery Pepper makes me shiver!

Sally led Prince into the middle again, and even though I was the only one not having a canter, I didn't feel so bad after what she'd said.

Oh great, it's time to prepare for afternoon lessons! Even if I can't canter, caring for Prince really cheers me up!

Tuesday, before tea

I CANTERED!

It wasn't very good, but at least I actually did it!

It was the afternoon lesson and after Tess and Lucinda had cantered to the back of the ride, Sophie went round and she did really well. Then it was my turn. "Good luck, Poppy," I heard Sophie say from behind me. It made me feel better to know she wasn't still upset with me. Still, my hands were trembling and I felt sick. I made myself pick up rising trot then sat down at the corner but I didn't use my legs to ask for canter, so of course I didn't get it.

"Never mind," called Sally. "Go rising down the long side and try again at the next corner…"

I nodded and went rising. At the next corner I sat again and this time I slid my outside leg back. Prince made the transition, but as soon as he did I had a complete panic and tensed up. I was bobbling about with my hands too high and my feet shooting forward, and I started feeling like I was going to fall off again. Poor Prince didn't know what to do with all the mixed signals so he cut off the corner and dropped back into trot. Sally called out, "Good try, Poppy! Right, we'll end there, I think!"

And that was it. It wasn't very tidy and it was only for a few strides, but I actually cantered! It's a long way from here to show jumping comps, of course, but it's a start!

Our afternoon lecture was about "points of the horse" – markings, colours, conformation and all that. We had this really fun game in two teams where we had to pick out the right colour and marking cards for these made-up ponies the other group described. All the girls were acting normal with me again, and Jennifer

was quieter than usual and
looked a bit sheepish.

Jennifer
looking
sheepish!

I have this feeling Jody
may have had a talk to
them when I was in the loo before lunch.
When we had to pair up to go round the
stables and note down all the different markings
we could find, Sophie grabbed my hand and
said, "Bags I'm with Poppy!" which felt really
lovely.

I still haven't actually spoken to Jennifer,
though. And she hasn't spoken to me — but at
least it doesn't feel like everyone's against me
any more.

Tuesday, in bed after lights-out

I'm using Millie's torch to see the page – hee hee! I just wanted to quickly write down that Jennifer and I are talking again.

At the table tennis tonight, Johnny put me and Jennifer together as a team – I think that was his sneaky was of trying to make us be friends.

At first I pretended that I had a twisted ankle and couldn't play, but after a while I got really into it (I can get very competitive, according to Mum!). In the end, I forgot that I was in a mood with Jennifer, and then when Jody brought the drinks out we started properly talking.

Of course, it was mainly Jennifer telling me how wonderful she normally is at table tennis and how she wasn't that good tonight because the table was the wrong kind, but at least it was better than frosty silence. I haven't exactly forgiven her, but staying in a mood won't make my holiday much fun either. Still, there's no way I'll ever tell her a secret again!

Tomorrow we're taking a trip to an actual ranch to meet Western Bob, who's going to teach us about Western riding. I've never done it before and I think it'll be really cool! Time to get some sleep now, so I'm ready to be a cowgirl!

Night, night
sleep tight!
Sweet pony dreams
till morning light!

Wednesday at 11.10am
- in the minibus going to Western riding (yee-hah!)

After our morning pony care and a lecture on feeding and stable management, it was time to get in the minibus. And the best thing is two Sunnyside ponies are coming with us as they've been trained in the Western style. One is Fisher, Amanda's pony, and the other is ... PRINCE!

None of us have ever done Western riding before, so we are all madly excited. Jennifer just now said she's seen some on TV, on *The Stables*, so of course she's acting like a complete expert – and scaring the younger girls by saying we'll have to gallop around lassoing huge cows! But Millie laughed and said she'd been loads of times and of course we won't! I'm stopping writing now as Jennifer is peeping over my shoulder.

Wednesday evening,
sitting on my bed writing this

What a fantastic day – and I loped (that's Western for cantering!). I've offered to go last in the shower so I can hang around up here and write in my Pony Diary. I'm desperate to get everything down before I forget one tiny detail because Western riding is AMAZING!

And Western Bob was brilliant, too! I didn't think he'd actually *look* Western, but he did! He wore a checked shirt and jeans with worn-in brown leather chaps that had fringes down the side, and a cowboy hat. He even *sounded* American.

Yee-hah!

First he introduced himself and asked all our names, then he explained that we were going to have a talk about Western riding, a Western-style riding lesson, and then a cook-out with Western mounted games afterwards. It sounded great and we all got even more excited!

We went into the barn and the ponies and horses were all in their own pens. Jody and Lydia unloaded Prince and Fisher from the trailer and Western Bob showed Amanda and I where to put them. With his beautiful piebald coat, Prince fitted right in with the Western ponies! Then Western Bob showed us the different tack they use in Western riding and how to tack up on this lovely pony called Nickle, who was an Appaloosa. He had amazing striped hooves and was really friendly. Western Bob told us that Appaloosas were first bred by native American Indians too

Nickle's striped hooves

— so Nickle really is a wild western boy!

There was this funny bit where Western Bob said, "Then secure the throatlatch," and Jennifer called out, "You mean throat lash," just like that.

"No, I mean throatlatch," said Western Bob, with a twinkle in his eye. "That's what we call it in Western riding – as I just told y'all!"

Jennifer got a bit sniffity then – she likes people to think she knows everything.

Then we played a really fun game called Quick Draw where Western Bob pointed to parts of the bridle and saddle and we had to go in pairs and beat each other to saying their Western names. I was up against Millie and she kept pretending to draw pistols on every go and saying things in a Western voice. In the end we had to abandon our turn because we were laughing so much.

After that, it was time to tack up our ponies. Western Bob had some special tack for Prince, which he brought over and hung on the railings of the pen.

I said, "Wow, it's amazing that you have the perfect tack to fit Prince."

Western Bob smiled and said, "Well, I'll tell you a secret – Prince used to live here before he went to Sunnyside." He patted Prince's neck and added, "We're old buddies, aren't we, fella?" Prince snorted happily – he likes Western Bob as much as I do.

So at least one of us knew about Western riding – phew!

The Western saddles were really heavy and we worked in pairs to swing them over our ponies' backs.

I thought we'd wear cowboy hats like Western Bob but we had to wear our normal crash hats that we'd brought with us. Then it was time to mount up and get moving!

It was really cool because instead of Group A and Group B we were all riding together because we were ALL beginners at Western riding.

First of all we walked around learning the new way of sitting and the different aids. The stirrup felt bigger and wider round my foot than normal and you have them very long in Western riding, so it felt like my legs were dangling way down. The steering is quite weird too, because you have to do neck reining, and none of us could get it right at first. You're not meant to pull on the bit but instead you use the reins against the pony's neck to turn him. Also, you're supposed to hold the reins in only one hand, but as we were beginners we started off with two. Even then we were all messing it up by moving our reins too far across, so we ended up twisting in the saddle and pulling our ponies' mouths. We were all going the wrong way, except Amanda, who seemed to be a natural, and Millie, of course, who'd done it before. But the ponies were lovely (Prince was a star as usual) and we started getting the hang of it in the end.

Then Western Bob asked us all to dismount and re-check our girths, which are called cinches in Western riding. We all stepped down

because the high cantle makes it impossible to swing your leg over and jump, but Jennifer tried to do just that and got stuck halfway!

Everyone was giggling and she looked really cross.

April said, "But I thought you knew all about Western Riding, Jennifer. That's what you said in the minibus."

Jennifer finally struggled out of the saddle and down to the ground. "Yeah, well, this is a different *style* of Western," she muttered.

I saw Western Bob smile knowingly at Jody but he didn't say anything. I liked him even more then.

Then we tried sitting to the jog, which is like sitting trot, only slower than normal. I really enjoyed it and I wasn't bouncing around at all, unlike poor Sophie and Tess! Also, I felt really safe with the high cantle and horn around me. Western Bob said I had a good seat and asked me to show the rest of the group how it was done. Everyone gave me a clap afterwards and I went red again, but this time with happiness.

Jody told me later that my years of experience had really shone through then. I've been thinking about it all day, and I can't stop smiling to myself. In fact I am beaming about it right now

After a while Western Bob said, "Okay, who wants to try loping?"

I said yes loudly with everyone else, but I didn't realize that loping is Western for canter – I thought it meant lassoing.

As Western Bob explained how to move from a jog into a lope (which is almost the same as asking for canter), I was getting more and more nervous, and trying to catch Jody's eye. I know I managed a few strides yesterday, but I still wasn't feeling confident about it – especially not in front of Jennifer.

Suddenly Jennifer pointed at me and said, "Excuse me, Poppy won't want to do this because she had a fall and…"

Western Bob raised a hand and she instantly stopped talking. He came over to me and gave Prince a pat. Then Jody got everyone else to walk on while we had a private talk.

"Poppy, I really think you can do it," said Western Bob. "You have a great seat and you're so in tune with Prince. Just relax and let everything else follow from there. Do you want to give it a try?"

I took a deep breath and nodded.

Western Bob grinned.

I joined the back of the ride and waited for my turn. No one was getting it right away and that made me feel much better. When it was my go I sat to the jog and tried to relax, then asked on the corner and suddenly it happened – I was cantering (well, loping!).

I felt comfortable and safe in the Western saddle and I just relaxed and went with Prince's movements. He seemed to know exactly where to go, so steering wasn't a problem. When I reached the back of the ride, I couldn't help looking over at Western Bob. He was looking at me too – with a wink and a smile! We had two more goes at loping before the lesson ended and I loved every second of it.

Afterwards, we had a yummy cowboy cook-out with sausages and beans, and this strange not-very-nice combo called biscuits and gravy that cowboys used to eat. Then we remounted for some Western games. And guess what? Amanda and April were the captains and they BOTH wanted me in their team!

We had a go at barrel racing and then we played a relay game where you have to pick up flags. I was so busy concentrating on getting the Western steering right and weaving round the barrels and grabbing the flags that I didn't even think about the fact that I was loping. I was just doing it.

And I felt really pleased when Amanda put me up against Millie, because she obviously thought we were the same kind of standard and I had a chance of beating her. I never dreamt I'd be doing so well this week – and it's all because of Prince!

I'm so lucky I got him.

When we got back it was nearly time for tea but I begged Jody to let me walk Prince down the ramp of the horsebox and up to the field. When it was just us I gave him a big cuddle and thanked him for being such a fab pony. "Without you, I'd still be scared to even trot!" I told him. "You've given me my riding back!"

Prince tossed his mane then, looking very proud!

It was cool because we were given these ribbons on pins for doing well at the Western ranch and I'm wearing mine right now, on my PJs. I'm going to wear it when I ride tomorrow too, to give me the courage to carry on cantering!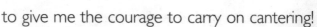

Oops, Jody's just come in and said absolutely everyone has been in the shower and they all went downstairs ages ago and if I don't hurry up I'll miss my hot chocolate – so I'm going right now!

Still Wednesday night, after lights-out

I'm writing this with Millie's torch again!

Amanda and April came into our room after hot chocolate and we were all chatting about the Western riding. They were saying how well I did today, and being really encouraging, and instead of feeling embarrassed, I was just pleased that they were being so nice. In fact, I don't know why I was so scared to tell everyone about the fall, and I kind of wish I'd been honest from the beginning. (But there's no way I'm admitting that to Jennifer!)

Then April and Amanda asked Millie if James (her big bro) has a girlfriend! Millie went, "Urgh, gross!" really loudly and we all burst out laughing (except Jennifer, who was acting a bit sniffity for some reason).

Talking about James made me think of my brother Luke, and Mum and Dad too. I'm really looking forward to seeing them again on Friday when they come to the gymkhana. I just hope the progress I made today sticks when I'm back in an English saddle. But I think that as long as I have my

FAB!

Prince, I'll be fine!

When Amanda and April had gone back to their own room and it was lights-out, I thought we'd be doing our usual silly whispering and telling ghost stories and jokes and stuff, but instead Jennifer said, "Well, I don't see why we bothered learning Western," in a sulky voice. "It won't help us improve our normal riding."

"Of course it will!" I cried. "It really helped my confidence and—"

"Shhh!" went Millie.

"Sorry," I whispered. "And anyway, Jennifer, not everything's about competition and improving. Some things can just be for fun. Like the gymkhana!"

Jennifer did a kind of snort and said, "Don't be so silly, Poppy. The gymkhana is going to be 100% competitive. Still, you won't be able to win anything on Prince because he's so slow, so maybe it's best if you just try and enjoy it for fun."

I felt instantly sick then. This time I knew that she *meant* to be nasty to me.

"Jennifer, what's wrong——" I began, but she just jumped out of bed and flounced off to the bathroom. Millie whispered, "Don't take any notice of her! She's just cross because she really worships April and Amanda and they only complimented *you*. She's jealous!"

69

When Jennifer came back I tried to keep my voice from going wobbly and told her, "If you're my friend you should be happy that I'm doing better now."

I thought she'd say sorry straight away but instead she turned and hissed at me, "First you used your fall to make everyone feel sorry for you, and now you're some kind of expert on Western riding!"

I couldn't believe that! "I was NOT trying to make people feel sorry for me!" I shouted. "I didn't even want anyone else to know. And it was YOU who told them! And it was YOU who claimed to be the expert on Western riding, not me!"

"Shhh!" went Millie, again.

"No more noise, girls!" Jody called up the stairs.

Jennifer didn't say anything after that. Instead she just huffed and puffed about, making the whole bunk bed shake, but after a while it stopped so I guess she must have fallen asleep. Soon Millie had too. I was so tired, but I couldn't sleep – I kept thinking about what had happened. I hate falling out with people, even if it's not my fault. But I feel a lot better now I've put everything down in here. There's no way I'm being friends with Jennifer any more – not after she said those things.

Anyway, I'm going to forget about her and close my eyes and think about my lovely Prince.

Thursday breaktime

This morning we've been having a Road Safety Lecture and getting our ponies ready to go on a hack out. It's a lovely hot day and I really want to enjoy it, but I'm very nervous as well, because it'll be the first time I've ridden out since my fall.

When I was tacking up just now I whispered my worries to Prince and I could feel him promising not to go galloping off with me, or dump me in a bush or anything. But still, I'm planning to stay close to Sally and Millie so they can help me out if I get panicky. I am also going to stay away from Jennifer because I am NOT her friend after what she said last night!

Thursday, about 9.45 pm, after lights-out

I've been trying to write in here all evening, but I've been on washing up duty and then we had a video night and now it's bedtime! I can't believe it's my last night here, or what happened out on the hack today!

When we left the yard, I was tucked in behind Amanda on Fisher near the front of the ride. Sally was leading and Lydia was bringing up the rear. Jennifer was behind me in the line somewhere but I was trying not to think about her and just concentrate on the ride instead.

I felt quite scared riding on the road, but we had our fluorescent bibs on and we kept in single file. I tried to think about what Western Bob had said about relaxing and being in tune with your horse and I sat deeply in the saddle and calmed down. Still, I felt really relieved when we signalled and turned up a track.

Prince felt ever so springy when we were trotting along the bridle path, and I could tell he was enjoying himself. We even had a canter up one of the hills and it was great because I went with his rhythm and trusted him. I wasn't even thinking, *Hands down, sit up* or anything – it just sort of happened on its own.

As we were going along this lovely part of the track next to a wood, Sally trotted up beside me and said, "You've done so well this week, Poppy. You've really given it your all and you're back on track. I'm very proud of you, and your family will be too."

I thought of Mum and Dad and Luke seeing me in the gymkhana and it really made me grin. "Thanks, but it's all down to Prince really," I told her. "There's no way I could have done it without him." I'm sure he heard because he did a big snort and shook his head and Sally and me both laughed!

"Let's just say you make a great team," she chuckled.

But, typical — Jennifer was listening in on our conversation and when I was telling Sally how great Prince was, she called out, "Yeah, if you like going steady."

"Well I do," I said firmly, forgetting that I still wasn't talking to her after last night.

Jennifer said, "Well, fine, but if you want to carry on improving, Poppy, you need more of a challenge. And so do I. In fact I think I've outgrown Flame."

Sally laughed and said, "Excuse me, who's the instructor round here? Poppy is doing just fine and there's still a lot Flame can teach you."

"But everything's easy for me," Jennifer whined. "Like, I bet I could even jump that log pile." She gestured towards a stack of logs by the edge of the wood. I thought it was just another brag – until she kicked on and took off towards the pile!

"Don't even think about it," Sally shouted. "You don't know what's—"

But Jennifer just picked up canter and started turning Flame towards the pile.

"Come back here!" Sally ordered.

Jennifer still didn't take any notice. She was heading straight for the logs, kicking on. Flame rushed at them and as she jumped, Jennifer threw herself forward really dramatically, much more than she needed to. Flame clipped the top log and it rolled off the pile, pulling others with it. The poor pony was totally spooked and stumbled on her landing, sending Jennifer tumbling down her neck and on to the floor. We all watched in horror as Flame cantered off into the woods, her reins trailing along the ground.

Millie leaped off Tally and held Lydia's horse while she ran into the woods after Flame. Sally was over by Jennifer in a flash but Jennifer didn't move or even moan and groan when Sally checked her over. I realized from my own fall that it was the shock. Then she suddenly got up and brushed herself down, trying to smile.

We all sighed with relief.

But Sally was furious. "You didn't even check what was on the other side, or whether the pile was stable, did you?" she shouted. "You deliberately disobeyed me! You were extremely lucky to get away with just bruises, Jennifer. You could have broken your neck!"

"I knew what I was doing," Jennifer began. "I just—"

"You put your horse in serious danger, and now she's loose in the woods with her reins dangling!" Sally shouted.

It all sunk in then and Jennifer started to sob hysterically.

Sally just stood with her arms folded, furious.

But – thank goodness! – Lydia came out of the trees leading Flame! Seeing that she was okay, Sally softened a little. "Right, well, I hope you've learnt a valuable lesson," she told Jennifer sternly. "Now on you get and we'll head back to the yard."

Lydia led Flame up to Jennifer and offered her the reins, but Jennifer backed away. "I can't!"

Sally sighed. "Jennifer, that fall was your fault, not your pony's. Now please get back on."

But Jennifer just snivelled and sobbed and shook her head. "I can't," she repeated, "not on *her*, anyway!"

Then the most awful thing happened. Jennifer whirled round and stared hard at me. "I want to go on Prince!" she whined.

I dropped forward and clung to Prince's mane. "No way," I said. "He's mine!"

Next thing, I heard Millie telling Jennifer, "You can have Tally, I'll ride Flame." I caught her eye and smiled my thanks. I knew she was saying it so I wouldn't have to give up Prince. But it didn't work because Sally just said, "Thanks, Millie, but I don't think your lovable thug would do Jennifer much good right now."

Sally looked at me hopefully, but I shook my head. How could she even ask?

Jennifer started sobbing again and I hugged Prince's neck fiercely. I couldn't give him up – I just couldn't! But there was real fear in Jennifer's eyes – she was terrified of Flame. Despite how horrible she'd been to me, I knew how important it was to get back on as soon as you can. I wiggled my hand up under my body protector and felt my Western ribbon, pinned to my fleece – somehow it made me feel braver. The next thing I knew, I was saying, "Okay, you can have Prince, but only for the ride home."

"Thanks," sniffled Jennifer. I dismounted and handed the reins to Sally, who mouthed "Thanks" at me. Then came the hardest part — riding Flame! After all, she was a whole hand higher than my Prince. And she's not just called Flame for her glossy chestnut coat — she has a fiery nature too! How would I control her? Would I dissolve into panic again? My head was spinning with scary thoughts.

Sally gave me a leg-up and I adjusted the stirrups. I took some deep breaths and tried to sink deep into the saddle. We all set off again and soon picked up trot. Flame seemed to have completely forgotten her stumble and was raring to go. I had to check her with my half halts and focus on keeping a good seat and strong leg contact. I felt a creeping panic in my chest that she might be about to bolt off, so I tucked her in firmly behind Prince, knowing he wouldn't give her any encouragement! Still,

Flame kept trying to break out, really testing me. I remember thinking that, despite her bragging, Jennifer must be a good rider to have managed Flame so well all week.

After a while she seemed to settle and I really started to relax. "I'm doing it," I kept thinking. "I'm riding a different pony – and it's okay!" We came to an uphill bit of the track and Sally asked everyone if we were all right for a canter. She looked especially at me and to my surprise I found myself nodding. I realized that I really wanted to go for it, even though I wasn't on my trusty Prince.

And then we were off! Flame absolutely bombed up the track, galloping at one point, and overtaking everyone except Lydia on her liver chestnut, Fly.

"You okay?" she called, as we thundered along.

BRILLIANT!

"Yeah!" I called back, and I realized I really truly was!

Back at the yard, Jennifer came over to swap ponies and the most amazing thing happened — she actually said sorry to me! "You didn't have to lend me Prince," she added. "Especially after how I acted last night. I'm really grateful, Poppy. Now I understand how you felt after *your* fall. It can be really scary!"

I could have stayed angry with her, but I was feeling great after the amazing canter (well, gallop, more like!) so I just said, "It's okay."

So all in one day I've made up with Jennifer and ridden a different horse than Prince and been out of the yard on a hack, and had a big canter (and gallop!). And now I'm definitely going to sleep because it's the gymkhana tomorrow and I want it to come as soon as possible.

At home on Friday, after tea and a long soak in the bath

It's so strange to be in my own room again and I'm really missing my new friends – even Jennifer. I'm missing Prince too, of course – but at least I've got his photo here, propped up against my lamp. I'm buying a proper frame for it first thing tomorrow. I'm going to write about the absolutely amazing thing that happened in the gymkhana today, so that I never forget it!

When we were getting our ponies ready (there was a tack and turnout class too, so we were all grooming like crazy and cleaning our tack), Jennifer came up to me and said, "You can have Flame for a couple of races if you like, so you'll be fast enough to win something at least."

I started feeling annoyed with her again for putting Prince down, but then I reminded myself that she was only trying to help – in her own way. So I gave Prince a big pat and said, "No thanks, I

don't mind if we don't win anything, I just want to enjoy riding my lovely pony!"

Jennifer shrugged and said, "It's up to you, but it really is all about winning, you know."

I just smiled and got to work on Prince's fetlocks with the dandy brush. I used to think winning was all that counted too, but I don't any more, not after what Prince and Western Bob have taught me. "Actually I think it's about being in tune with your pony and having fun," I told her.

She just laughed. "Okay, Poppy, whatever you say. Can you pass me the hoof oil?"

So I did, and it was good to be friends with her again. It's funny how she still says annoying things, but they don't seem to annoy me so much any more – weird!

When we'd finished getting our ponies ready they all looked great, in their different ways. Lovely had about twelve pink ribbons in her tail and Amanda had given Fisher chequer-pattern quarter marks. Amita even did this amazing crochet plait thing on Rupert, but I kept Prince quite plain. He's a bit cobby for mane plaits, and anyway at heart he's a wild western boy, not a show pony! So I just gave him a really thorough groom and shined up his coat with a damp cloth and some conditioning spray. I couldn't resist winding some ribbons round his brow band, but I chose blue and green, so that he looked very smart and not girly at all.

Ribbons

Mum, Dad and Luke came and found me in the yard when we were lining up to use the mounting block. Mum said, "So what's the news, Poppy? We haven't heard from you all week! I hope that's a good sign!"

I laughed and said, "Yep, a very good sign – you wait and see!"

Before we started, Johnny judged the tack and turnout competition, and gave first prize to Sophie and Monsoon. They really deserved it too – Monsoon looked amazing with her mane all plaited up and her tail full of ribbons! Amanda and Fisher scooped second, and Amita won third. I knew Prince didn't mind about not being placed – getting poshed up just isn't his thing.

Amanda and Fisher

Sophie and Monsoon

Amita and Rupert

The gymkhana games were brilliant – I even picked up a second in the bending race. Jennifer romped home in the sock race, which is when you go as fast as you can back and forth collecting socks to put in a bucket. With Flame's speed they were a sure thing to win. Amanda won the agility test, with twelve round-the-worlds in one minute. And Sophie got drenched in the apple bobbing. She just couldn't get hold of her apple and ended up taking her hat off and sticking her head right in the bucket. Even though everyone had finished and ridden back to the start line, she still wouldn't give up. She strapped her helmet back on, mounted up and rode back, wet hair all dripping in her face. Lucky for her that the tack and turnout competition was BEFORE that!

Afterwards, we had a break for a drink and
biscuits, and I was chatting with Millie when
Jennifer came up to us. She said well done for
the bending, and I said well done about the sock
race. It's so nice that things are okay between us
again. Then Amanda and April came up and
asked me whether *Luke* has a girlfriend.
While I was busy saying, "Urgh! Gross!"
Millie cried, "Hey, I thought you liked *James!*"

They looked at each other and squealed,
"We do ... AS WELL," then ran off giggling.
Honestly, there's no way I'll ever get boy mad
like that. I'll only ever care about ponies!

Soon we remounted for the last competition
– the Chase Me Charlie. As we lined up in the
arena, I touched my Western pin, which I'd
transferred on to my show jacket. I needed all
my courage not to bow out. I never thought I'd
be jumping this week – but no way was I sitting
it out!

89

The first jump was a tiny cross pole I could have popped with my eyes closed before the fall, but I was just as nervous as the other Group A girls who'd only been over a few poles on the ground. Lydia led them over, then it was my turn. I took it slowly too, approaching in trot and only squeezing Prince into canter on the last few strides. He pretty much stepped over, and it was no big deal to anyone else – but to me it was everything! Mum and Dad looked completely amazed too.

Suddenly it wasn't just a little gymkhana game – I really wanted to win. I stayed as focussed and determined in each round as I would have been in a novice-class show jumping competition.

Tess was first to be knocked out, on Tiny, followed by Sophie and April. Jennifer rushed the third round and brought the pole down. After a couple more rounds only me, Millie and Amita were still in. We were all amazed when Amita made a bad approach and sent the top pole flying! That only left me and Millie!

As Sally was putting the pole back up, Millie grinned at me. "So it's down to us two again," she said. "You beat me last time, in the show jumping. But you won't beat me at this!"

I gave her a big grin back. "Wanna bet?"

We both cleared the next round and the poles went up again to almost a metre. It was really tense and the spectators were all cheering us on – I could hear Dad bellowing, "Come on, Poppy!" Tally's smaller than Prince but he's also got a bolder jump, so it was fairly even in the pony stakes. It was all down to our skill – and nerve.

I was up first. I picked up canter and then came straight at the middle of the jump, using the manège fence as a guide. I kept a steady, even pace and then spurred Prince on at the last minute, encouraging him to give it that bit extra. And, of course, being Prince, he did … and we cleared it!

Looking grim and determined, Millie pulled Tally round and belted at the jump. She took off well but Tally left a leg slightly behind on the landing and knocked the pole! I stared at the fallen pole and it took a moment to sink in.

We'd won! We'd actually won!

Mum, Dad and Luke all went completely wild, even though Luke is normally too busy being cool to look excited about anything! Millie rode over to say well done and when we leaned across to shake hands, she added, "It'll be third time lucky for me, you'll see. Next time I'm up against you, watch out!"

millie ↘   me ↘

I grinned. "So there'll be a next time?"

"I hope so," she said. "If you start competing in shows again."

I smiled at her then, because I knew I would. Then it was time to go home, and I know this sounds strange, but it was really sad saying goodbye to Jennifer. She lives in Manchester so I probably won't see her again. But I didn't mind saying goodbye to Millie because I know I'll be meeting up with her at an event very soon — and beating her, if I have my way!

Sunnyside isn't that far away, so I might even be able to visit Prince sometimes too. I told him that when I said goodbye and it cheered him up a tiny bit (although he was still really sad about me going home). I stroked his ears and ruffled his mane and whispered, "I've got my confidence back and it's all thanks to you, Prince. You're the kindest, most patient pony I've ever met and I'll never forget you!"

Sunnyside Stables

I never, ever thought I would say this, but
Jennifer was right – about one thing, anyway. I
AM ready for some new challenges. I really
believed I could only ride Prince, but I managed
fine on Flame. And now I can't wait to get back
to my local stables and start learning new things
and riding different ponies, even Pepper! And
although I'll really miss Prince, I'm glad he's still
at Sunnyside, ready and waiting for the next
person who needs him.

For Jodie Maile and the fab young riders
of Goulds Green Pony Club Centre.

With huge thanks to our cover stars Ella and Cracker Jack,
pony guru Janet Rising and all at Ealing Riding School.

www.kellymckain.co.uk

STRIPES PUBLISHING
An imprint of Magi Publications
1 The Coda Centre, 189 Munster Road, London SW6 6AW

A paperback original
First published in Great Britain in 2006

Text copyright © Kelly McKain, 2006
Inside illustrations copyright © Mandy Stanley, 2006
Cover photograph copyright © Zoe Cannon, 2006

ISBN: 978-1-84715-007-3

A CIP catalogue record for this book is available from the British Library.

Printed and bound in the UK

6 8 10 9 7